The New Adventures of Postman Pat

Postman Pat™

and the suit of armour

John Cunliffe

Illustrated by Stuart Trotter

from the original television designs by **Ivor Wood**

Hodder
Children's
Books

a division of Hodder Headline plc

More Postman Pat adventures:

Postman Pat and the hole in the road
Postman Pat in a muddle

First published 1996
by Hodder Children's Books,
a division of Hodder Headline plc,
338 Euston Road, London NW1 3BH

Story copyright © 1996 Ivor Wood and John Cunliffe
Text copyright © 1996 John Cunliffe
Illustrations copyright © 1996 Hodder Children's Books
and Woodland Animations Ltd.

ISBN 0 340 678062
10 9 8 7 6 5 4 3 2 1

One morning, Pat spotted a new poster on the wall of the village post office.

"Now then, what's this?" he said. "Garner Hall, open to the public? Well, it will be a lovely show . . ."

"That's right, Pat," said Mrs Goggins, "but think of all the cars and coaches, and the litter! Suppose you got stuck in a traffic-jam, with all this post to deliver?"

"It'll take more than that to stop me," said Pat.

"Miss Hubbard asked if you'd pop in and have a word with her," said Mrs Goggins. I don't know what she wants."

"I expect it's something to do with Garner Hall," said Pat. "I'll not forget. Cheerio!"

Pat was on his way.

"I hope she doesn't want a hand with her blooming bees," he said. "I remember last time - 'Keep still,' she said, 'and they won't sting you'!"

When he arrived at her cottage, he knocked at the door.

"Come in, Pat!" called Miss Hubbard.

When Pat went in, the wind went in with him. It whooshed round the room. There were piles of books and papers everywhere, and the papers blew and fluttered about.

"Goodness me, Miss Hubbard, whatever are you doing?" said Pat. "Ooops, what a wind! It's like a paper storm! Look out!"

He tried to catch the papers and put them straight, but only made things worse. He knocked a pile of books over, and Jess jumped out of the way only just in time.

"For heaven's sake, man, shut that door!" said Miss Hubbard.

"Ooops-a-daisy! Oooh, sorry!" said Pat.

"I wouldn't like to sort this lot out . . ."

"Don't worry, Pat," said Miss Hubbard. "I'm just getting ready for the opening of Garner Hall. The Major has asked me to show people round, and I must find out all about the old times in Greendale."

"Oh, yes, I saw the poster," said Pat. "Well, I don't know that all that much has happened in Greendale. No famous battles, no ghosts, nothing like that."

"Don't be so sure, Pat," said Miss Hubbard. "You never know what you'll find. Tell you what, there's one thing I would like to see. Folks say Granny Dryden has a very old diary that her granddad kept, and *he* was head butler at Garner Hall! Now, I don't suppose she would let *me* have it, but if *you* were to ask her, she might just lend it . . ."

"It's worth a try. I'll ask her when I call with the letters," said Pat.

"I feel sure she'll let you have it," said Miss Hubbard. "Do please ask her. I'll take good care of it. I'm off to Garner Hall now, to have a good look round."

"I'll pop in when I've finished my letters," said Pat, "and let you know how I got on."

"Good man! Bye for now! I'll see you at the Hall."

"I nearly forgot your post!" Pat laughed. "Cheerio!"

Pat was on his way. His next stop was at Ted Glen's.
"Hello, Ted!"
Ted could not hear Pat. He was making such a noise with his power-sander. Pat shouted as loud as he could.
"TED!"

"Hey up, Pat!
How are you doing?
Nay, I'm not deaf - no need
to shout! Look at this!
Just like new! All ready for
the grand opening . . ."

"I know," said Pat,
"at Garner Hall! Is it an
old suit of armour?"

"It is an' all," said Ted.
"The Man in the Iron Mask!
What do you reckon, Pat? I've
always fancied trying one on . . ."

Pat gave Ted his letters and said,
"Now's your chance. I'll bring a
tin-opener next time I call,
just in case you get stuck . . .
Here's some *mail* to go with it!
Cheerio!"

Pat was on his way . . .
His next stop was at Granny Dryden's cottage.
"Now then, what was it that Miss Hubbard wanted?" said Pat.
"I think she said it was an old diary. Hello! Anybody at home?"

Granny Dryden had a big black book in her hands.

"Oh, there you are, Pat," she said. "Now, just look what I've found.
Ee, it takes me back, seeing these old pages, all brown and faded.
Wilfred's very words, just as he wrote them at Garner Hall all that
long time ago."

"I never saw anything like it," said Pat. "What a show it would make at Garner Hall! Do you think I could borrow it, so that Miss Hubbard can make a few notes, for when she shows folks round?"

"Well, I can't make it out properly with my glasses," said Granny Dryden, "so you might as well have it."

"I'll take good care of it," said Pat. "It'll be safe with me. And it will be wonderful for people to see it, in the place where it was written. Bye, Granny Dryden!"

It was time for Pat to be getting along to Garner Hall. Miss Hubbard would be waiting for him and the precious diary.

He arrived at Garner Hall at last. Major Forbes was at the door, looking out for him.

"Come along, Pat," barked the Major. "I see you've got it. Miss Hubbard's waiting for you . . ."

"Pat! Good man!" shouted Miss Hubbard. "And the diary!" She began riffling through the pages at once. "Now, let me see, there *must* be something interesting here . . ."

They could hear a strange sound coming along the passage. It was like a hundred tin cans going for a walk. In came Ted Glen with with the suit of armour!

"Where do you want this, then?" said Ted.

"Over here, Ted," said the Major.

What a clattering and clashing Ted made with that armour! He seemed to think it was a new kind of jigsaw-puzzle.

"Just about my size, I reckon . . . let's see . . ." he said to himself.

Pat didn't wait to see what Ted did next. He was just creeping out quietly, when Miss Hubbard heard him. "Is that you, Pat? Come along here and look at this diary! "What's wrong with it?" said Pat. "Wrong? Wrong, Pat? There's not a thing in it that I can put in my story of Garner Hall. It's just - just - boring. Look!" "Hmmm . . ." Pat read a bit out. "'It was a nice day today . . . went fishing . . . caught three trout . . . white bread for tea . . . went to bed early . . .' Well, yes, I see what you mean. Nothing very historical about that." "*Historical*? Oh, Pat, it makes me feel *hysterical*! Look, I haven't got a single note on my paper, not a thing!"

At that moment, something hard crashed into the door, followed by all kinds of grunts and growls.

"Ooooh! Ummfff! Grfffff!"

In the banqueting hall, Ted was blundering about in the suit of armour! A muffled voice wailed from inside.

"Help! Get me out of here! I'm stuck! Get a tin-opener! I can't see where . . . Oooooooh . . .!"

There was another huge crash as he walked into a table.

In the library, Pat and Miss Hubbard heard heavy footsteps going along the passage and out of the front door.

"Did you hear that, Pat?" said Miss Hubbard.
"The ghost of Garner Hall is going out into the garden!"

"Bless us all, whatever . . . whoever . . . er, um," said Pat.
"Yes, I think I know . . ."

Miss Hubbard dashed outside without waiting for Pat. He went to look for Major Forbes.

Outside, the suit of armour was
blundering about all over the
garden like a mad robot. It went
straight through a prize
rose-bush,

and through a pond and
two flowerbeds, then crashed into a tree.

Then it was off again, and soon
disappeared behind the greenhouse.

Pat and Major Forbes came out, just in time to miss seeing it. The Major was saying to Pat:

"Did you say, Pat, did you say *my suit of armour*? What? Eh? Speak up, man!"

"Well . . . er . . . yes, Major, I did say . . ." mumbled Pat. "I *think* so . . ."

"Out here? In the flowerbeds? Parading about?" shouted the Major.

"Yes, Major, I think so . . ."

"But it should be in its special place in the Hall where Ted put it!"

"I know, Major," said Pat, "but look at your flowers . . .! All crushed and spoilt . . .!"

"Badgers! Foxes! Deer!" shouted the Major. "No stopping the blighters! That's what it is! You're dreaming, Pat. There's no suit of armour out here . . .

"Stop, man - Listen!"

There was
a trampling
sound, far away.
"Sounds more like
an elephant," mumbled Pat.
"A whole herd of them if you ask me, Pat!"
"I think it's gone back inside!" said Pat. "Come along, Major!"
"This way! Follow me!" bellowed the Major.

Back in the hall, the suit of armour was leaning against the wall, trying to unscrew its head.

Pat and the Major ran back indoors. There was a thump, and a crunch, and rattling footsteps not far away.

"I'm sure I heard something in there," said Pat. But when they ran into the room the noise came from, it was empty!

"Where can it be now?" moaned the Major.
"Do you think we've had burglars, Pat?"
There was a strange noise in the next room. A thump, a crash, and then a sliding-scraping sound. They ran in to see. Was it a ghost?
Pat whispered, "Look!"

There was a dark opening in the wall. The old panelling had slid back to show a secret passage. Pat went to see what it was.

"Slowly does it . . ." said Pat, feeling his way. The Major could hear his voice coming out of the darkness.

"It's dark in here, ouch!
Has anybody got a torch?
Ooooh, what's that? Help! Oh!
There's an iron man, a horrid robot,
a— oh, it's . . . I think it's, it's . . . is it you, Ted?"

Slowly, the suit of armour came out of the darkness. Its helmet was off now, and there was Ted's grubby face looking out.

"Erm . . . hello, Major - hello, everybody," said Ted. "Sorry about the noise and - erm - the mess. I must have panicked . . . wish I'd never tried the blessed armour on . . . just fancied it . . . got stuck. Couldn't see where I was going . . ."

But Pat had come out with a great bundle of musty old papers in his hands.

"Look what I found!" he said. "It might be just what Miss Hubbard needs!"

"Is it treasure?" said the Major.

"Let me see," said Miss Hubbard. "This looks like treasure of a kind. And a secret passage as well! Just think what a thrill that'll be for the visitors! They'll flock in when they hear about it. These papers look super. All the history of the house - ghosts, escapes and robberies, battles, a visit from the Queen - everything!"

"All thanks to Ted," said Pat.

"And the suit of armour," said Ted. "I would never have found the secret door if I hadn't crashed into that panelling."

"I wonder if there are any naughty secrets about the Forbes family in here?" said Miss Hubbard. "You never know what skeletons there might be in an old cupboard."

"Hmmm . . . well . . . never mind about that, eh, what?" said the Major. "Time for tea! Come along everybody!"

They all went to the kitchen and had a feast of scones and cream and raspberry jam, with steaming cups of tea, and a plate of sardines for Jess.

The suit of armour stood quietly in its corner. It never moved again. When Garner Hall was opened to visitors, everyone who came, from grannies to first-year infants, had to be told the story of the day the armour went for a walk, and found the secret door.